MONI MONSTER
MEETS INGA
THE GIRAFFE

G. MAY

FREE BONUS:
Moni Monster Coloring Book

If you>d like to get our free printable 10 page

Moni Monster Coloring Book, you can download it

here by clicking on this link:

https://lp.apexauthors.com/7191/moni_monster_series_/index.html

Early every morning, a friendly, green, giant beast named Moni Monster visited Inge, a beautiful and young giraffe who lived freely on the plains of the African savannah.

"Hi-ya, Inge," Moni Monster said happily, "You look a little worried today, is something wrong?"

"I think I hear a shuffling sound coming from inside this hole," Inge replied, not looking away from the hole.

2

Inge and Moni Monster looked down, and something jumped at them.

"Snake!" Inge cried, galloping away so fast that she almost tripped on her long legs.

Moni took a closer look and, with a laugh, shook his head as a small warthog's face looked up from inside a burrow in the ground.

"I got ya good!" The warthog said to Inge, who frowned at him.

"What's your name, little warthog? Where is your family?" Moni Monster asked.

The little pig-like animal replied, "My name is Worty."

"Do you know it's very dangerous for a warthog piglet to be alone on these grasslands?" Moni Monster asked.

Worty shrugged, "My family chased me away because I am always playing tricks on my sisters and pranking my brothers."

"What kind of tricks?" Inge asked, still frowning at the piglet.

Worty giggled, "Sometimes when my sisters are asleep, I put spiders next to them. It's very funny to see them scream and jump up and down when they wake up."

8

"Oh yes," Worty continued, "I also like play-fighting with my brothers when they want to sleep and putting sticky tree glue on my parent's beds so they can't get up when they wake up!

But this morning I wanted to really frighten the other warthog piglets, so I roared so loudly that my family thought there really was a lion nearby. They were terrified and scattered all over the place. It took my mother hours to gather everyone up. She was very angry, and she told me to go away and think about all the trouble I caused." Worty finished with a lowered head.

10

Inge clicked her tongue in disapproval.

Moni Monster shook his head and said, "Yes, your mother was right. That was a silly trick to play on your family, especially when there are many dangerous, hungry animals here on the grasslands."

Worty's eyes widened as he blurted out, "Careful, look over there, there's a..."

Inge spun around so fast that her legs tangled, and she fell to the side, landing head first in a tree.

Worty squealed and rolled over with laughter at the sight of Inge with a bird's nest on her head.

Okay, Worty, this is not a good place for another practical joke," Moni Monster said.

When Moni Monster had helped Inge put the nest back in the tree, they walked to the waterhole.

Worty Warthog stared up at Inge and said, "My goodness! You must be the tallest animal in the world; I bet you can see forever!"

"Yes, giraffes are some of the tallest," replied Inge. "Because I can see far ahead, I can warn other animals when there is danger. I can also eat the delicious leaves on the tree-tops. My size helps me stay safe."

"How about you Worty, how do you keep safe?" Inge asked.

"I have big strong tusks, so I can defend myself against anyone who tries to hurt me, see?" Worty replied, holding up a tusk.

18

When they reached the waterhole, Worty Warthog went down on his elbows to drink. Inge spread her long, elegant legs so that she could sip the cool water.

As they drank, Worty saw a massive crocodile slowly swimming towards Inge.

Worty squealed as loudly as he could in warning, "Inge, run, run as fast as you can! A crocodile is coming for you!"

Inge shook her head; she believed Worty was playing yet another trick on her and did not listen to Worty's warning.

Worty kept on squealing, and as Inge leaned down for another drink of the refreshing water, she quickly realized that Worty was not joking. She watched in horror as the cold-blooded animal swam towards her.

Inge was frozen with fear, and her legs would not move.

Crocodiles are speedy swimmers, and before she knew it, the crocodile was right in front of her!

22

Moni Monster leaped into the water, "Run away!" Moni Monster yelled to Inge as he picked the reptile up and tossed it a long way back into the water.

The crocodile spun and spun through the air. When the crocodile landed in the water, it was so dizzy that it swam in circles, chasing its tail for a few seconds.

Worty laughed from the shore, making the Crocodile look up. When it saw Moni Monster, it swam away so fast that it almost looked like it was standing upright and running on water.

"That was cool! Did you see that Crocodile go!?" Worty laughed.

Inge trembled; she had a narrow escape. Moni Monster tried to comfort her by saying, "There is no need to be afraid, Inge. I will always protect you from danger."

Worty Warthog's eyes were huge as he looked at Moni Monster with admiration. He could not believe how Moni Monster's incredible speed and strength had saved Inge.

28

When Inge finally recovered from the shock, she turned around to Moni Monster and said in a grateful voice, "Thank you for saving me from the jaws of that big scaly crocodile."

Moni Monster replied, "I'm here to make sure no harm comes to any animals on the savannah. But Inge, I think you should thank Worty instead."

Inge turned to Worty and said, "Thank you, Worty."

Worty Warthog grinned and asked, "Do you want to join me in a good wallow in some squishy mud?"

"Ew!" said Inge, "I will not join you in the mud, but I hope you visit me often."

Worty smiled, "I will, and I'm sorry for pranking you earlier."

"From now on," Inge said, "I'll check to make sure there are no hidden dangers before I go near the waterhole."

"And from now on, I'll stop playing pranks on my fellow warthogs," Worty said, then he winked and added, "Well, maybe just a few tricks so no one is bored."

"Worty, you're hopeless," Moni Monster said, shaking his head and smiling in a grandfatherly way. "You can always have a bit of fun, just remember never to put your family or other animals in danger."

"Can I join you on your next adventure Moni Monster?" begged Worty.

Moni Monster bent down and putting his hand on Worty's back said, "Sure, as long as you have been a good piglet."

Made in the USA
Las Vegas, NV
05 March 2021